KATIE KAZOO, SWITCHEROO

It's Snow Joke!

Mrs. Smith

58

For Amanda, my actress—NK
For Stefan, we'd tell you why, but it's
a secret; we promised not to tell—J&W

GROSSET & DUNLAP
Published by the Penguin Group
Penguin Group (USA) Inc., 375 Hudson Street,
New York, New York 10014, U.S.A.
Penguin Group (Canada), 90 Eglinton Avenue East, Suite 700,
Toronto, Ontario, Canada M4P 2Y3
(a division of Pearson Penguin Canada Inc.)
Penguin Books Ltd, 80 Strand, London WC2R 0RL, England
Penguin Ireland, 25 St Stephen's Green, Dublin 2, Ireland
(a division of Penguin Books Ltd)
Penguin Group (Australia), 250 Camberwell Road,
Camberwell, Victoria 3124, Australia
(a division of Pearson Australia Group Pty Ltd)
Penguin Books India Pvt Ltd, 11 Community Centre,
Panchsheel Park, New Delhi - 110 017, India
Penguin Group (NZ), Cnr Airborne and Rosedale Roads,
Albany, Auckland 1310, New Zealand
(a division of Pearson New Zealand Ltd)
Penguin Books (South Africa) (Pty) Ltd, 24 Sturdee Avenue,
Rosebank, Johannesburg 2196, South Africa

Penguin Books Ltd, Registered Offices:
80 Strand, London WC2R 0RL, England

Text copyright © 2006 by Nancy Krulik. Illustrations copyright © 2006 by
John and Wendy. All rights reserved. Published by Grosset & Dunlap, a
division of Penguin Young Readers Group, 345 Hudson Street, New York,
New York 10014. GROSSET & DUNLAP is a trademark of Penguin Group
(USA) Inc. Printed in the U.S.A.

Library of Congress Control Number: 2006002434

ISBN 0-448-44396-1   10 9 8 7 6

It's Snow Joke!

by Nancy Krulik • illustrated by John & Wendy

Grosset & Dunlap

Chapter 1

"Okay, now all the forager ants can start searching for food!" Mr. Guthrie told the kids in class 4A.

Katie Carew giggled as she began looking along the windowsills for the treats Mr. G. had hidden around the room.

Katie's fourth-grade class was studying animal behavior. Some classes might read books about how ants lived. But that wasn't the way Mr. G. taught. In his class, the kids were pretending that they *were* ants in a colony. They were all wearing wire antennae on their heads. And they had each been given an antlike job.

"Okay, once you forager ants have

gathered the food, bring it back to the center of the room," Mr. G. said. "Then the queen, the nursery worker ants, and the ants that are in charge of cleaning up waste can have a snack. But remember, anybody who is a patrol ant will have to wait. You can't eat while you're guarding the colony."

"Hey, that's not fair!" George Brennan shouted out. He was a patrol ant. "I want a snack, too."

"You'll get one," Mr. G. assured him. "But you can't leave your post. Suppose a bird was coming near the anthill. You'd have to warn the others."

George frowned, but he stayed at his post near the classroom door.

"Hurry up, forager ants," Mandy Banks said. She adjusted the gold crown on her head. "It takes a lot of energy for me to lay enough eggs to keep this ant colony going!"

Katie giggled. Mandy sure loved being the queen ant.

"Once everyone has eaten, the ants who are on clean-up patrol should get rid of the waste—which means picking up all the candy wrappers and throwing them in the trash," Mr. G. told the kids.

"In a real ant colony, getting rid of waste means getting rid of dead bodies," Kadeem said. "I read about that on the Internet."

"Ooo, yuck," Emma Weber groaned. She was one of the ants who was supposed to clean up. "I think I just lost my appetite."

"More for *me*," Emma Stavros, a forager ant, told her. She popped a snack-size chocolate bar into her mouth.

"Man, I wish I was a forager ant," George groaned from the doorway.

Katie stared at him. "Don't say that!" she exclaimed loudly.

The kids all stared at her.

"What's with you?" Kevin Camilleri asked.

Katie gulped. She hadn't meant to shout. It was just that Katie hated wishes. She knew how much trouble they could cause when they came true.

What were the kids doing?

Chapter 2

It had all started last year, when Katie was in third grade. She had had a miserable day. First she had lost a ball game for her team.

Then she'd fallen into the mud and ruined her new jeans.

Worst of all, she'd let out a giant burp, right in front of the whole class. The kids had really teased her about that.

It had been one of the most embarrassing days of her life. And that night, Katie wished to be anyone but herself. There must have been a shooting star flying overhead, because the very next day the magic wind came.

The magic wind was like a powerful tornado

that blew just around Katie. It was so strong
that it could turn Katie into somebody else!
One, two . . . switcheroo!

The first time it happened, the magic wind
had turned Katie into Speedy, the third-grade
class hamster! Katie spent the whole morning
going round and round on a hamster wheel
and gnawing on chew sticks!

The magic wind had come back many times
after that. Sometimes it changed Katie into
other kids, like her friend Jeremy Fox. Other
times it turned her into grown-ups she hardly
knew, like Cinnamon, the woman who owned
the candy store in the Cherrydale Mall. What
a mess *that* had been! Katie had accidentally
sent candy hearts with mean messages to
some of her friends at school. She'd almost
ruined Valentine's Day forever!

Another time, the magic wind had turned
Katie into Lucky, Jeremy's kitten. She'd had
to lick herself clean—which meant swallow-
ing pieces of kitten fur. *Blech.* Even worse,

Katie's own dog, Pepper, had chased her up a tree.

That was why Katie didn't like wishes coming true.

"I . . . um . . . just meant that you shouldn't wish for a different job, George," Katie said, trying to explain her outburst. "Every ant helps the colony."

"That's exactly right, Katie!" Mr. G. said, his antennae bouncing up and down. "No ant would ever wish to be anyone else."

Katie sighed. Ants were smarter than they looked.

What happened
To Katie at the start?

? _____ ?

Chapter 3

"That was so much fun," Kevin Camilleri said as he and the other kids in class 4A left the school building at the end of the day.

"So is this," Kadeem Carter added as he held out his tongue and tried to catch some of the snow that had just started to fall.

"Mr. G. had so many treats for us to find," Katie agreed.

"And eat," George reminded her. He rubbed his belly. "Those Peppermint Patties were really good, weren't they, Katie Kazoo?"

Katie grinned. She loved when George called her by the way-cool nickname he had given her back in third grade.

"I didn't want to give up that crown,"

Mandy admitted. "It was awesome being queen for a day."

"You guys are so lucky," Jeremy Fox said. "We're studying animal behavior, too. But we're doing research projects in the library."

Katie gave her friend an understanding smile. Jeremy was in the other fourth-grade class—4B. His teacher, Ms. Sweet, was very, very nice. But she wasn't as interesting as Mr. G. The kids in class 4A definitely had more fun than the kids in 4B.

"Searching for candy is way more fun than writing note cards on how sharks live," Becky Stern remarked as she stuck out her tongue to catch a few snowflakes.

Suzanne Lock shook her head. "Well, I think writing reports is very grown-up," she told the kids. "I love doing research. I'm an expert now on how animals hide from their enemies. They do it by blending in with their background. It's called *camouflage*. C-A-M-O-U-F-L-A-G-E."

"We know how to spell, Suzanne," Jeremy

groaned.

Suzanne rolled her eyes. "Anyway, it's very interesting. I think the stuff you guys do in 4A is for babies."

Katie scowled. Suzanne was one of her best friends, but sometimes she could be mean— especially when she was feeling jealous . . . like now.

"Why is writing reports grown-up?" Kevin asked her. "We did reports back in *kindergarten*—on dinosaurs, remember? Sounds like *you* guys did baby stuff today."

Suzanne stuck out her tongue. But not to catch a snowflake. She stuck it out at Kevin. Kevin stuck his tongue out at Suzanne.

Katie frowned. Now *everyone* was acting like babies. "I'm sure we'll have to write a report soon, too," Katie assured Suzanne. "We just got to do something different today, that's all."

"Hey, you guys," George interrupted. "Maybe it will snow really hard."

"Cool!" Kadeem cheered. "You think school

will be closed tomorrow?"

"I don't know," Katie told him. "It has to snow an awful lot for that to happen."

"If it snows hard, I'll get to wear my new parka. It has white fur around the hood," Suzanne boasted.

Katie stared at her in surprise.

"Relax, it's *fake* fur," Suzanne assured her. "I've got white snow pants, too. And white boots. When I wear it all together, I can pretend I'm a polar bear blending in with the snow. That's camouflage."

"We know, Suzanne," Kevin told her.

"I hope we get lots and lots of snow," Jeremy remarked. "I want to take out my snowboard. I'm getting pretty good on it."

"I'll bet you're great!" Becky Stern told him. She smiled widely.

Jeremy blushed and turned away. "It's cold out here," he said. "I'm going home."

That afternoon, Katie sat in her room and tried to do her homework. But it was hard. She kept looking out the window at the snow. It sure would be nice to get a chance to go sledding.

Brrriiing.

"Katie, can you get the phone?" her mother called up to her. "I'm busy."

Katie hurried down the stairs to the kitchen and picked up the phone. "Hello?" she said.

"Katie Kazoo, you'll never guess who this is!"

Katie smiled. She knew exactly who it was.

The voice on the other end of the phone was one of the most famous voices in the whole world. It belonged to Rosie Moran, a famous child actress.

Katie had met Rosie last year when Rosie was filming a movie in Cherrydale. Since then they'd been sending each other postcards and e-mails all the time.

Rosie didn't know it, but Katie had almost ruined her career. It hadn't really been Katie's fault. The magic wind had turned her into Rosie, and Katie had to act out a scene in the movie, instead of Rosie. And Katie was no actress. She was terrible!

"Hi, Rosie," Katie said happily. "How are you?"

"I'm great. And you're never going to believe this!" Rosie exclaimed. "I'm at the Pine Mountain Ski Resort!"

"Pine Mountain!" Katie shouted into the phone. "That's right near here!"

"I know!" Rosie squealed back. "I'm filming

a movie called *Diamonds on Ice*. It's about a group of jewel thieves. There are a lot of snow scenes in the movie. We couldn't film them in Hollywood, so we came here!"

"Wow. Your school is on break already," Katie said. "You're so lucky."

"Katie, you're missing the point," Rosie told her. "I'm right near you. Maybe this weekend, you could come to Pine Mountain. You could go skiing while I'm on the set. And then we could hang out together."

"Oh, that sounds awesome!" Katie said excitedly. "Let me just ask my mom."

"Ask me what?" Mrs. Carew wondered as she carried a big basket of laundry down the hall.

"It's Rosie Moran!" Katie told her mom. "She's making a movie at Pine Mountain. She wants to know if I can come visit this weekend."

Mrs. Carew thought for a moment. "I have to work at the bookstore on Sunday," she said.

"But I don't see any reason why we can't go to Pine Mountain on Saturday."

"Yipee!" Katie shouted right into the phone.

Rosie giggled. "I guess that means you can come."

Chapter 4

By the next morning, there was a beautiful blanket of white snow on the ground. But not enough for school to be closed. So Katie put on her red boots, her thick pink parka, her wide wool scarf, her hat, and her mittens, and headed off to school.

When she got to the playground, she saw that everyone else was all bundled up, too. She could hardly tell who was who. Nobody's faces were showing.

But Katie just *had* to find Jeremy. She had something really important to ask him. Finally she spotted his yellow parka near the slide in the middle of the yard.

"Jeremy, hi!" Katie called out as she raced to catch up with him.

"Hi," Jeremy replied. "What's up?"

Katie looked around, making sure no one—especially Suzanne—was near. "Do you have a soccer game tomorrow?" she asked him.

Jeremy shook his head. "The game's on Sunday this week."

"Oh, good!" Katie exclaimed. "Do you want to come to Pine Mountain with me tomorrow? You could bring your snowboard!"

Jeremy looked down. "I . . . um . . . I know I kind of told everyone I was a great snow-boarder, but I don't really know how to ride that thing," he admitted. "I mean, I can go down little hills in the park and stuff, but on a ski slope . . ."

"That's okay," Katie assured him. "You don't need to bring your board. We can ski instead. I've never been skiing. We can take a class together."

Jeremy's face brightened. "That sounds like a great idea," he agreed.

"Then afterward we'll hang out with Rosie Moran," Katie continued. "She's at Pine Mountain filming a movie."

"You sure she won't mind if I come with you?" Jeremy asked.

Katie shook her head. "No. Rosie likes you. She likes everyone from our school."

Jeremy laughed. "Well, *almost* everyone. She wasn't too crazy about Suzanne *Superstar*!"

Katie giggled, remembering the last time Rosie was in town. The kids were all going to have tiny parts in her movie. But Suzanne had renamed herself Suzanne Superstar and tried to get herself a really big role. Instead, she'd gotten herself thrown off the set!

"That's kind of why this has to stay a secret," Katie explained. "I bet Suzanne would want to come with us if she knew Rosie was making another movie."

"Okay. I promise I won't say anything,"

Jeremy assured her. He looked around quickly. "Don't worry. There's no one around to hear us."

But someone was nearby, and *had* heard. Suzanne was under the slide the whole time. She was all in white and she did blend in with the snow—just like a polar bear.

A polar bear with a very angry face!

Ding-dong.

"I'll get it," Katie shouted excitedly as the doorbell rang early on Saturday morning. "It must be Jeremy!"

But when Katie opened the door, it wasn't Jeremy's face staring back at her. It was Suzanne's.

"Hi, Katie," Suzanne said.

"Suzanne, what are you doing here?" Katie gasped.

"I'm going with you to Pine Mountain," she said simply.

"What?" Katie asked her.

"I *said* I'm going with you today," Suzanne repeated.

"How did you know about Pine . . ." Katie began.

"My mother called your mother and asked if I could spend the day with you. And your mother said yes."

"B-b-but . . ." Katie stammered. Suzanne sure worked fast. Katie's mom hadn't even had time to tell her.

"What's the matter? Don't you *want* me to go with you?" Suzanne asked, narrowing her eyes.

"Uh . . . sure," Katie said. "It's just that we're going to see Rosie Moran, and you and Rosie don't always get along."

"Oh, I bet we'll get along fine," Suzanne told her as she walked into the house. "It won't be like last time. I'm sure Rosie isn't jealous of me anymore."

Katie frowned. Rosie jealous of Suzanne? That wasn't exactly the way Katie remembered it. But there was no point in arguing with her. Suzanne would never admit that she was jealous of anyone.

Just then, Jeremy came hurrying up the walk. "Sorry I'm late," he said. "I couldn't find my other boot." He stopped for a minute and stared at Suzanne. "What are you doing here?" he asked her.

"Going to Pine Mountain," she answered triumphantly. "With you and Katie."

Chapter 5

"Katie Kazoo!" Rosie Moran shouted the minute Katie entered her trailer. The actress leaped up out of her makeup chair and hugged her friend.

Katie was amazed. Rosie had really grown. She was the same age as Katie, but now she was at least three inches taller. Her face, however, looked exactly the same. But her hair . . . Katie began to giggle.

"What's so funny?" Rosie asked her.

"You are," Katie told her. She pointed to the big mirror in the middle of the trailer. "Look."

"Oh, no!" Rosie groaned. "I look ridiculous.

Katie giggled harder. Rosie *did* look ridiculous. Only half of her hair was brushed. On one side of her head, Rosie's brown hair had been brushed and combed until it was long, straight, and shiny. The hair on the other side of her head was a tangled mess of chocolate-colored curls.

"We haven't finished yet," the tall, thin man standing near the makeup mirror explained.

"This is Raul," Rosie told Katie. "He's the hairstylist for the movie."

"Hi," Raul said. "Rosie's going to look fantastic when we're finished. I promise."

"I'm sure she will," Katie told him.

"I can't believe you're actually here," Rosie said to Katie. "I've really missed you."

"I missed you, too," Katie told her.

"I have to work until about three o'clock," Rosie said. "But after that, we can have a snack at the ski lodge. And maybe we can go to the arcade, too."

"Cool!" Katie agreed.

"I'm just sorry you have to go skiing by yourself until I'm finished working," Rosie said sadly.

"Oh, I won't be alone," Katie assured her. "I brought Jeremy and . . ."

"Great!" Rosie interrupted her. "He's a lot of fun."

Katie nodded. "I also brought Suzanne," she added, looking doubtfully at Rosie.

Rosie bit her lip to keep from laughing. "You mean Suzanne *Superstar*?" she asked.

Katie nodded. "I sort of had to."

"It's okay," Rosie said. "She's kind of funny. Where are they?"

"They're with my parents in the lodge having hot cocoa," Katie said. "They'll be here in a minute."

No sooner were the words out of Katie's mouth than the door to the trailer opened. A blast of cold air rushed in, bringing Jeremy and Suzanne with it.

"Wow. It's cold out there," Jeremy said.

"Hi, Jeremy," Rosie said.

"Hey, Rosie," he replied. "Cool hair."

Rosie giggled. "Katie liked it, too," she said. Then she turned to Suzanne. "Hi, Suzanne. I love your ski outfit."

"Thanks." Suzanne spun around so Rosie could get a good look at her white parka, white pants, and white boots. Then she turned her attention to Raul. "Hi," she said, holding out her hand. "I'm Suzanne. You must be Rosie's director. Well, today's your lucky day. One day I'm going to be a big star, and you can say how you met me."

"Uh, Suzanne," Rosie began. "He's not . . ."

"Oh, don't worry, Rosie," Suzanne said. "We won't ever be competing for the same parts."

"No, that's not it," Rosie tried to explain. "It's just that Raul isn't . . ."

But Suzanne wasn't listening. "Would you like me to read something for you? Because I know I would be great for this film."

"Why?" Jeremy whispered to Katie. "Is it a horror movie or something?"

"Shhh," Katie whispered back. She turned to Suzanne. "Um, Suzanne. Raul isn't who you think he is."

"What do you mean?" Suzanne asked.

"I'm the stylist," Raul told her.

Suzanne frowned. "Oh," she said quietly.

"It's okay," Rosie told her. "Anyone might

make a mistake like that. Don't be embarrassed."

"I knew that he wasn't the director," Suzanne told Rosie. She forced a smile to her lips. "I was just acting. My character was a girl who wanted to be in a movie. And I had you all fooled. See what a good actress I am?"

"Great," Jeremy remarked, rolling his eyes. He looked over at Katie. "It's getting hot in here. Let's go over to the bunny slope and see if it's time for our lesson."

"Good idea," Katie agreed. "Come on, Suzanne."

"But I thought maybe I could stay here and . . ." Suzanne began.

Katie shook her head. "Oh, no. Remember what happened the last time you tried to get into one of Rosie's movies?"

Suzanne frowned. There was no arguing with that. "Fine," she harrumphed.

Katie breathed a sigh of relief as Suzanne headed for the door. Now Rosie wouldn't have to worry about what Suzanne might do or say next. And Katie was about to learn how to ski!

This was going to be a great day. Katie was sure of it!

Chapter 6

"Come on, Katie!" Jeremy shouted as he headed for the bunny slope.

Katie gulped. She did not like the look of the hill. For something called a bunny slope, it sure looked steep to her.

"I . . . I don't know . . ." she said nervously.

"You can do it," Jeremy assured her. "Just think of it as a really cool roller coaster."

"You're not *chicken*, are you?" Suzanne asked.

Katie frowned. She hated when people said she was chicken. And there was no way she was going to let Suzanne make fun of her—especially not after Suzanne had invited herself on this ski trip. It wasn't like Katie had wanted her along.

"Okay," Katie said, following Jeremy up the hill to where their lesson was going to start. It was hard work clomping on skis. Katie fell down twice.

As they reached the top of the slope, Katie looked down. Suddenly she felt really wobbly. "I'm not sure I can do this," she whispered to Jeremy. "Maybe I should go to the lodge and wait for my parents to finish skiing."

"You can do it," Jeremy assured her again. "We're going to learn together, remember?"

"Well, *I'm* certainly not going to fall," Suzanne told Katie. "I'm very graceful. It's something you learn when you take modeling lessons."

"I wish she'd take pantomime lessons," Jeremy whispered to Katie. "Then she'd have to keep quiet."

Katie giggled. Usually Katie felt bad when her two best friends said mean things about each other. But today Katie didn't care what Jeremy said about Suzanne. After all, Suzanne wasn't being nice. And there was no reason for it.

Or was there a reason? Had Suzanne figured out that Katie had invited Jeremy and not her? Suzanne always got upset if Katie left her out of anything.

But it wasn't really Katie's fault. She *would* have invited Suzanne—if Suzanne didn't act so weird whenever she was around Rosie.

The other beginning skiers in the class were gathered around a small woman in an orange parka. Katie tried to follow her friends over to the group. Unfortunately, she fell down again. The small woman, who had long, brown hair, hurried over and helped Katie to her feet.

"Thanks," Katie murmured as she wiped the snow from her ski pants.

"No problem," the woman said with a smile.

Katie looked more closely at the woman's bright orange parka. The words *Ski Instructor* were written on the back. Katie frowned. Her ski teacher had already seen how clumsy she could be.

Suddenly, a little boy standing beside Katie began to cry. "I'm cold, my nose is running, these ski boots hurt, and this hill looks scary," he wailed.

Katie knew exactly how he felt.

"Johnny, just wait until you start skiing," his dad assured him. "You're going to want to do it again and again."

"No, I won't!" Johnny howled.

The small woman with dark hair bent down, lifted up her blue snow goggles and smiled at Johnny. "Hi, I'm Lola," she said. "I'm your ski instructor."

Johnny turned his back to her.

"I'll let you in on a little secret, Johnny," Lola continued gently. "This is my very first day as a ski instructor. So we're both doing something new. Isn't that cool?"

But Johnny didn't think that was cool. He just kept on crying.

So Lola stood up and, keeping a smile on her lips, said, "Hey, everybody! Are we going to have fun?"

"Yes!" the class cheered.

"No!" Johnny shouted.

"I'm going to show you everything you need to know to begin skiing," Lola told her students. "And then, after your lesson, we'll all go to the lodge and have a cup of hot chocolate."

At the mention of hot chocolate, Johnny stopped crying.

Lola smiled at her group of students. It wasn't a big group. Just Jeremy, Suzanne, Katie, Johnny, Johnny's little sister, Johnny's dad, and an older woman in a green, fake-fur parka.

"Okay, now let's get started," Lola said,

using her ski poles to help her make her way to the front of the crowd. "First we're going to learn to do the snow plow." Lola placed her skis so that the tips were close together and the ends were wide apart. "It may seem hard at first, but before you know it, you'll be zooming down to the bottom of the hill."

Katie gulped. *Zooming?* "Jeremy, I can't do this," Katie said. "You know how clumsy I am. I'll break my leg if I do this. I'll probably break both legs!"

Johnny looked up at Katie. "I don't wanna break my leg," he wailed.

"Me neither," his little sister cried out. Now she started sobbing, too.

Lola looked at Katie and shook her head. "I wish you hadn't said that," she told her. "You're making these kids really nervous."

"I . . . I didn't mean to," Katie told her. "But *I'm* really nervous."

"I wanna go home!" Johnny cried loudly.

"Me too!" his sister chimed in.

Their father sighed. "Maybe my kids are too young for this," he told Lola. "I'm taking them back to the lodge. Can we get a refund on our lessons there?"

Lola nodded. "Of course, but . . ."

The father took off with his children. Katie bit her lip. Lola had lost almost half the class! Katie tried to do what Lola showed them and held her poles the way Lola said. But all she could think of was how bad she felt. She hadn't meant to scare those kids. Finally, she turned and began trudging off toward the side of the bunny slope.

"Now where are *you* going?" Lola asked her.

"I'm going to see if I can get those kids to come back," Katie explained.

"But you can't leave now," Lola told her. "You're going to miss learning how to fall correctly."

"That's okay," Katie told her. "Falling is the one thing I'm good at already."

Chapter 7

"Excuse me! Please, wait up!" Katie cried out to Johnny's dad.

But Katie was clumsy on skis. She couldn't move quickly at all. So before she could catch up, Johnny, his sister, and his dad were out of sight.

"WAAHHHH!" Katie could hear Johnny's cries becoming softer and softer as he got farther and farther away.

There was nothing for Katie to do except stumble back to the class. But it was *so* hard to move in the snow.

"Come on," she said to herself. "You can do it. Right, left, right, left." Katie slid her legs back and forth on the snow. She was moving pretty well. And then . . .

Thump. She banged into a rock that was hidden in the snow. It knocked her off balance and she fell sideways between a couple of pine trees.

As she struggled to sit up, Katie blinked back a few tears. This day wasn't turning out at all like she'd expected.

And suddenly, it was getting much, much colder. A really cold wind began to blow. Katie pulled her scarf up over her mouth and nose and tried to keep warm.

But a scarf couldn't help Katie. Not now. After all, this was no ordinary wind. This was the *magic* wind. And a wool scarf was no match for that!

The magic wind began blowing harder and harder. It was like a fierce icy tornado, circling just around Katie. It blew harder and harder, chilling her right to the bone.

And then it stopped.

Just like that.

Katie Carew was gone. She had turned into someone else.

But who was she?

Slowly, Katie opened her eyes. She looked down at herself through blue ski goggles. She was wearing a bright orange parka.

Wait a minute. Katie didn't have blue ski goggles.

Or an orange jacket.

But Lola did.

Katie looked down at her feet. The plain rental skis were gone. A pair of shiny red skis were in their place.

Lola's skis.

Oh, no! Katie had turned into Lola—right in the middle of a ski lesson!

Katie didn't know how to ski. And there was no way she was going to be able to teach other people how to do it. Katie gulped nervously.

This was *so* not good!

Chapter 8

"Lola, can we ski down the hill now?" Suzanne asked. "I want to see how fast I can go."

"Um . . . well . . ." Katie stammered. "I don't think . . . I mean . . ."

"She's going to teach us the correct way to fall, remember?" Jeremy reminded Suzanne.

"Why?" Suzanne replied. "Katie's not here. She's the one who does all the falling."

Katie scowled. She certainly was here. Suzanne just didn't know it. Suzanne wouldn't be making fun of her if she realized that Lola was really Katie.

"That's not nice," Jeremy said.

Katie smiled. At least Jeremy was standing up for her.

"Yeah, well, it wasn't nice for you and Katie not to invite me to come skiing today," Suzanne answered. "I heard everything you two said while you were near the slide."

"But nobody else was there," Jeremy insisted. "I even looked."

Suzanne smiled proudly. "I was camouflaged in the snow. See, I told you it works!"

Jeremy frowned and kicked at the snow with his ski.

Suzanne turned to Katie. "I don't plan on falling, Lola. So can I just go?"

"Nobody plans on falling," Katie replied. "It just happens."

At just that moment, Katie's skis slipped right out from under her. "Whoops!" The next thing Katie knew she landed hard—right on her bottom—in a big mound of snow.

Jeremy, Suzanne, and the woman in the green furry parka all stared at her in amazement.

"You see, uh . . . well . . ." Katie began as she struggled to her feet. "You never know when you might slip. It can happen anytime, anywhere, and to anyone."

"Wow," Jeremy said. "That looked like it really hurt!"

"Yes, it did look painful," the woman in the furry parka agreed.

Katie rubbed her bruised rear end. Painful?

They had no idea.

The lodge at the bottom of the bunny slope looked so far away. How was she going to make it down the hill?

"You see," Katie told them. "You never know when you could fall and . . . WHOA!" Katie shouted out as she lost her footing again and headed downhill. "HEEELLLLP!!!"

Chapter 9

"Get out of the way!" Katie shouted out as she zoomed past skiers.

Katie slid faster and faster down the mountainside. "YIKES!" She turned, hoping to slow herself down. Instead, she skied through some trees and came out on a much steeper slope.

"Oh, noooooo!"

Ahead of her Katie could see the film crew and the actors. Her right ski hit a rock. She flew up in the air and twirled like an ice skater.

Katie landed on one leg just as a cameraman was taking a close-up shot of Rosie.

"HELP! ROSIE! PLEASE!" Katie screamed

as she soared past.

Rosie looked up at the sound of her name, but she didn't see anyone she recognized. After all, Katie didn't look like Katie anymore.

Katie zoomed on, moving faster and faster.

"Somebody stop me!" Katie called out as she flew over a bump and sailed in the air again. She shut her eyes. Over and over she flipped—one somersault, two, and then three.

Finally she rolled to a stop.

It wasn't until she stood up on solid ground again that Katie opened her eyes slowly and looked around. Somehow she had made it all the way down the hill not far from the lodge.

She glanced up to the right, at the bunny slope. She could see Jeremy and Suzanne standing next to each other with their mouths wide open.

"Ha ha ha!"

Katie turned her head suddenly. That little boy—Johnny—was pointing in her direction.

He, his sister, and his dad were standing outside the lodge with cups of hot cocoa in their hands.

"Lola's so funny, Daddy," Johnny said. "I changed my mind. I want to ski. Can we take a class with Lola now?"

Johnny's dad didn't say anything. He was too busy staring at Katie in amazement. "That was incredible, Lola," he told Katie. "I've never seen anything like that."

Neither had the head ski instructor of the Pine Mountain Ski Resort. He stomped out of the lodge and trudged through the snow to where Katie was standing.

"Lola!" he shouted angrily. "What was that about?"

"I . . . um . . ." Katie mumbled. "I tripped."

"Yeah, right. Championship skiers don't just trip," the head instructor insisted with a frown. "And why would you shout for help? Do you know that a guest called the emergency rescue crew?"

"I didn't mean to . . ." Katie began.

But he didn't want to hear any excuses. "We cannot discuss this here in front of our guests," he told Katie. "I am going to my office. I expect you to join me there in ten minutes."

As he stormed off, Katie gulped. Lola was in big trouble—*on her very first day of work.* And it was all Katie's fault.

All Katie wanted was to take off her skis. She trudged slowly toward the ski stand, taking care not to fall again. She didn't need any more people staring or laughing at her.

Actually, they were staring and laughing at Lola, which was worse. Lola was a champion skier—not a total klutz!

Katie was so tired. And walking in skis was so hard. She couldn't make it to the ski stand. She saw an empty bench, practically hidden by the trees.

Katie sighed as she sat down. What was she

going to tell Lola's boss, anyway? It wasn't like she could explain about the magic wind. He wouldn't believe her.

Katie wouldn't have believed it, either, if it hadn't happened to her.

Just then, Katie felt a cool breeze blowing on the back of her neck. She looked up. None of the trees were moving, even though the breeze was getting stronger.

Which could mean only one thing. This was no normal wind. The magic wind was back!

The magic wind started to blow faster and faster now, circling Katie like a tornado. It whipped around her, moving so hard and fast that she thought it might blow her away.

And then it stopped.

Just like that.

Katie Carew was back.

And so was Lola. In fact, she was sitting on the bench, right next to Katie.

"What? How?" Lola murmured looking

around. She stared at Katie. "How did I get down here? And what are you doing sitting next to me?"

"Well, I kind of fell and . . ." Katie began.

Lola looked puzzled. "The last thing I remember, I was about to teach the class how to fall down."

"You did," Katie told her. "Well, sort of. You kind of fell down the mountain."

Lola rubbed her back. "Well, that explains why I'm sore." She thought for a minute. "Did I fall all the way down the mountain?"

Katie nodded. "You also did some twirls and somersaults."

"I remember that. At least I think I do," Lola said, blinking her eyes. "It's all kind of fuzzy." She stopped for a minute. "Did anyone see me?"

Katie sighed. *Everyone* had seen her. "You made a lot of people laugh," she told Lola, trying to make her feel better.

It didn't seem to work. Lola seemed very

upset. "Okay, since you seem to know every-thing, why am I sitting here?"

"Your boss wants to see you in his office," Katie explained. "I think you were on your way over there."

"Carl wants me to come to his office? Oh, no!" Lola exclaimed. "That can mean only one thing. He wants to fire me!"

Katie gulped. Lola's first day on the job was going to be her last! This was *so* not good.

Chapter 10

"Katie, what are you doing sitting here?"
Rosie asked as she walked by a few minutes
later. "I thought you were skiing."

"I was," Katie said. She thought about her
big fall down the bunny slope. "Well, sort of.
Now I'm waiting here for the ski instructor."

Rosie shrugged. "Oh. Do you mind if I sit
with you?" she asked sadly.

"No, of course not," Katie said. She looked
at Rosie's frowning face. "Are you okay?"

Rosie shook her head. "Not really. I think
they're going to have to cancel the movie. And
it's not fair. I mean I've worked so hard and . . ."

"Cancel the movie?" Katie asked, surprised.

"Why would they do that?"

"Because my stunt double got the flu. We just got the call a minute or two ago. She's not going to be able to work for at least two weeks," Rosie told her.

"What's a stunt double?" Katie asked her.

"She is the woman who does all the skiing for me in the movie," Rosie explained. "They dress her up like me and then film her from far away. Onscreen it looks like I'm the one doing the skiing."

"Oh," Katie said. "Well, can't you just do your own skiing in the movie?"

Rosie shook her head. "I hardly know how to ski. My stunt double was going to do all sorts of flips and turns on the mountain."

"So why don't they just wait two weeks for your stunt double to feel better?" Katie asked.

"That would cost the movie company too much money," Rosie explained. "And I have to be back at school."

Just as Rosie walked off sadly, the lodge

door swung open. Lola came walking out. She looked very, very sad, too.

Katie figured she must have been fired. And that gave her one of her great ideas.

"Don't worry," Katie called after Rosie. "*Diamonds on Ice* isn't over yet! I have a plan."

Quickly she leaped up from the bench and started to run after the ski instructor. "Lola, wait!" Katie shouted out. "I have to talk to you."

Chapter 11

"Okay, let's try that wig on her," the director of Rosie's film told Raul. "And make sure it doesn't come off when she does the flip."

Lola smiled at Katie as Raul adjusted the wig. "Thanks so much for getting me this job," she said. "It really makes up for getting fired."

"Now you can be a stunt skier," Katie told her.

"It's not as good as being a movie star, but . . ." Suzanne began.

"What do you know about being a movie star?" Jeremy asked her.

Just then a real movie star entered the hair

and makeup trailer. "Hi," she said, holding her hand out. "You must be Lola."

Lola leaped up out of the chair with surprise. The wig slipped to one side. "Wow! You're Rosie Moran!" the skier gasped. "I can't believe I'm meeting you."

"That's me," Rosie replied. "And now you're me, too. At least in this movie!"

Katie stared in amazement as Rosie and Lola stood side by side in the trailer. Even though Rosie was a kid, and Lola was a grown-up, they looked a lot alike. For starters, Rosie was really tall for a kid, and Lola was pretty short for a grown-up, so they were almost the same height. They were also wearing the exact same green and white snowsuit and the same ski boots.

Katie could see how Lola could look like Rosie during the movie's skiing scenes. As long as the camera never showed Lola's face, the people in the audience would be fooled into thinking Rosie was really skiing.

"Okay, now here's the scene," the director told Lola. "Maxie—that's Rosie's character—is being chased by two jewel thieves who think she has a giant diamond sewed into the lining of her coat."

Lola nodded. "Got it."

The director pointed toward the top of a high ski slope, where two skiers were already standing. "Those two men are going to ski right behind you," he explained to Lola. "You have to zigzag between those trees, jump over the gray rock to the left, and then do a twist in the air before landing at the base of the mountain. Cameramen are planted at various points to film the scene."

Lola nodded. "Sounds easy enough."

Katie shook her head. "Not to me," she said.

"I'm so glad it's you and not me doing this," Rosie told Lola.

Lola left the trailer and put on her skis. Then she took the ski lift up to the top of the mountain. Two other stunt skiers, who were dressed as the robbers, stood behind her.

"Is everybody ready?" The director was speaking into a walkie-talkie to a cameraman at the top of the hill. "Okay. Rolling and . . . action!"

Whoosh! Lola took off down the steep mountainside at top speed. The two other stunt skiers took off after her.

Katie and her friends watched with amazement as Lola expertly zigged and zagged her way through the trees, leaped over the rock, and did a twist in the air—all in the few seconds it took for her to reach the bottom of the mountain.

"And . . . cut!" the director shouted out through his megaphone. "That was great, everyone. Take a breather and go on back up. Next we'll shoot the scene in which Lola skis right through the open doors of the lodge."

A few minutes later, Lola followed a cameraman toward the ski lift. The director turned to one of his assistants. "You'd better make sure they've cleared the lodge out for this shot," he told her. "We don't want any guests to get in the way of our filming."

Just then, Carl, the head ski instructor, strolled onto the movie set.

"That ski stunt was amazing," he told the director.

"Lola did a great job," the director agreed. "We were lucky to get her."

"Lola?" Carl asked, surprised.

"That's right," Katie said proudly.

"Well . . . I . . . um," Carl stammered. "I . . . er . . . certainly hope that when her name appears in the credits, it also says that she's an instructor here at the Pine Mountain Ski Resort," he told the director.

"But she's *not* an instructor here," Katie reminded him. "You fired her, remember?"

Carl forced a nervous smile to his lips. "That was just a joke."

"But Lola doesn't want her old job back," Katie said.

Suzanne stared at her in amazement. "She doesn't?"

Katie shook her head. "She's in show business now. She's a performer." She looked up at the top of the mountain, where Lola was getting ready to do her next stunt. "But maybe she'd agree to do her own ski stunt show every day."

"Her own show?" Carl asked. "I don't know about . . ."

"Then I guess she could do her ski stunt show at another ski resort," Katie said.

"Now wait a minute," Carl said nervously. "I didn't say no, yet."

"Lola could do the same kinds of tricks she's doing in this movie," Katie suggested. She smiled, remembering how Johnny had laughed when he'd seen Katie flip and flop down the bunny trail. "Lola's Ski Stunt Spectacular. It would be great for business."

"Lola's Ski Stunt Spectacular," Carl repeated. "I like that."

"And I think maybe she should get a raise, too," Katie continued. "She's going to be working really hard."

"Boy, Katie, you'd make a really good Hollywood agent," Rosie teased.

"Maybe I'll let you be my agent, Katie," Suzanne added.

Katie shook her head. Work for Suzanne? She didn't think so.

After she finished filming her next scene, Lola skied over to where Katie, Rosie, Jeremy, and Suzanne were gathered.

"Hey, Lola, great stunts," Carl greeted her. "Can't wait to see what else you come up with for the folks here at Pine Mountain."

Lola stared at him. She was very confused. "Here?" she asked. "I thought you fired me."

That's when Katie told her the good news.

Katie beamed as she watched Lola and her boss shake hands on the deal. Once again, Katie had proven that she could fix whatever mess the magic wind made.

"And now," Lola said, turning toward Katie, Rosie, Suzanne, and Jeremy, "it's time for you to have that ski lesson we never finished. Come on, I'll teach you!"

"Take that, magic wind," Katie whispered quietly under her breath as she and her friends followed Lola to the bunny slope.

Chapter 12

"I'm skiing! I'm really skiing!" Katie squealed with delight as she made her way down the bunny slope.

She couldn't believe it. She wasn't zooming down the hill at top speed or anything, but she was moving.

"This is so awesome," Jeremy shouted.

"Hey, wait for me!" Rosie called to Katie and Jeremy as she pushed off from the top.

"Rosie, please be careful," the director of her film cried out from the bottom. He buried his head in his hands and tried not to look as his star took a turn going down the side of the hill.

"See you guys at the bottom," Suzanne said as she shifted her body slightly to the side, moving past Katie, Jeremy, and Rosie.

"She's always got to be the winner," Jeremy groaned. He was skiing even slower than Katie was.

But Katie didn't care if Suzanne beat her to the bottom. Katie was just glad to be upright and not on *her* bottom!

Lola was a really good teacher. Not only was Katie skiing, but she wasn't scared of falling anymore. Lola had taught them all how to fall correctly so they wouldn't get hurt. The trick was to fall uphill on your tush. The kids had all had a good time flopping down backward in the snow to practice that.

Of course, Suzanne had boasted that that would never be something she'd have to do. She was positive she wouldn't fall.

But that didn't stop it from happening.

"WHOAAAA!" Suzanne shouted as she lost her footing and fell backward into the snow.

Suzanne was struggling to get back on her feet. But getting up was a whole lot tougher than falling down.

"Hold on, Suzanne," Lola called and took off from the hilltop. "I'm on my way."

When Katie, Rosie, and Jeremy reached Suzanne, Jeremy said, "Nice trip. See you next fall."

Rosie giggled. "That was a funny one, Jeremy."

Suzanne groaned.

Katie felt bad. Even though Suzanne had been kind of awful today, Jeremy shouldn't make fun of her. Falling could happen to anyone.

"You know what, Suzanne?" Katie said, trying to change the subject. "When I stand this way, all I can see is your face. Your whole body is camouflaged like a polar bear in the snow."

Suzanne smiled gratefully up at Katie. "And if I pull my scarf over my face you can't see me at all," she told her.

Just then, Lola skied over. "Okay, where's Suzanne?" she asked Katie, Jeremy, and Rosie.

Suzanne pulled the scarf from her face. "See, I told you it worked!" she boasted.

"That is pretty cool," Jeremy admitted.

"I'll say," Rosie agreed. "Like a special effect in the movies."

Lola smiled and reached out her hand. "Here, I'll help you up," she offered.

Katie grinned. It was really great that everyone was finally getting along.

As they skied the rest of the way down, Katie suddenly felt a cool breeze blowing on the back of her neck. She gulped nervously. Oh, no! Was the magic wind coming back again?

Was she going to switcheroo into someone else? Right now? In front of everyone?

Up until now, the magic wind had only come when Katie was alone. But there was no telling what the wind would do. Maybe this time it . . .

"Man, it's getting cold out here," Jeremy said suddenly. He pulled his scarf tighter around his neck. "That wind is really picking up."

Phew. Katie breathed a sigh of relief. It wasn't the magic wind at all. It was just a regular, everyday, run-of-the-mill kind of wind.

Which meant she would get to stay Katie Carew.

At least for now.

Soapy the Snowman

Katie and her friends never let a dreary winter day keep them from having fun. In fact, on really cold days, they just make their snowmen indoors. You can, too. Here's how to make your own Soapy the Snowman. (Have a grown-up help you using the toothpicks.)

You will need:
2 cups of mild, powdered laundry detergent
$1/2$ cup of warm water
Toothpicks
An electric beater
A mixing bowl
Twigs, buttons, a pipe cleaner, tiny beads

or birdseed, orange tempera paints, and anything else you'd like to use to give your snowman personality!

Here's what you do:

1. Pour the detergent into the mixing bowl. Add the water and mix it until the laundry detergent feels like dough. Allow the dough to sit for about five minutes.

2. Shape the soap dough into three balls.

3. Stack the balls. Start by gently pushing a toothpick halfway into the bottom ball.

4. Push the middle ball onto the top of that toothpick. Then repeat this for the third snowball, which will be Soapy the Snowman's head.

5. Now it's time to decorate your snowman! Start with his button eyes. Then add a row of small beads or seeds to give him a great smile. Twigs are terrific for arms. You can even paint a tiny twig orange and use it as a carrot nose. Let your imagination go wild!

When you are all finished, leave Soapy the Snowman alone to dry. It could take a few hours. But be patient. Soon you'll have a snowman pal who won't ever melt away!